Walk in Honour

Deng Garang Bul

Africa World Books Pty Ltd

A Note from the Publisher

The publisher wishes to acknowledge and thank Dr Douglas H. Johnson for his invaluable help and support for Africa World Books and its mission of preserving and promoting African cultural and literary traditions and history. Dr Johnson and fellow historians have been instrumental in ensuring that African people remain connected to their past and their identity. Africa World Books is proud to carry on this mission.

ISBN: 978-0-6485028-5-2

Design and typesetting: Africa World Books

Dear reader

If you have the desire and the passion for advancement, whether in your life or in the lives of others and you are willing to take the risk associated with it, your faith and your imagination can provide the lift you need to reach the intended destination.

Your faith and your imagination are your wings that can take you above or below the horizons. You can mould your vision into something remarkable and reach the heights you, and only you, can imagine. Alternatively, you can allow your thoughts to fail you – the choice is yours.

The Walk in Honour was an imagined advancement. While navigating the rough terrains – the hills and the mountains of the Northern Territory, I did not imagine a gloomy end but thrills. I endured the scorching heat with <u>HOPE</u> that was so invincible that it pushed me to the finish line. I walked to restore <u>HOPE</u> to the afflicted, the hopeless and the fatherless children of South Sudan, and you can too.

Introduction

In 1974, Dr Muhammad Yunus was struck by the level of poverty in his country of Bangladesh and lent $US27 out of his own pocket to forty-two poverty-stricken households who were earning money making and selling bamboo stools. Dr. Yunus expected only to get his money back. He was not out to make a profit but was being creative, seeking a way for these people to escape poverty. In this he succeeded. Dr. Yunus later had this to say:

> *My experience working in the Grameen Bank has given me faith; an unshakeable faith in the creativity of human beings. It leads me to believe that humans are not born to suffer the misery of hunger and poverty. They suffer now as they did in the past because we turn our heads away."*
>
> Dr. Muhammad Yunus, the founder of Grameen Bank.

His initial loan of $27 to poor women in Bangladesh led to the establishment of the Grameen Bank, a microfinance and community development bank founded in 1983. Grameen Bank now is worldwide, including a branch in Australia, and lends cash to the impoverished without requiring collateral.

The South Sudanese people, whether individually or collectively as a community, always gave voluntarily and generously. Put simply, they believed generosity to be a virtue admired and desired by all regardless of socio-economic status or material wellbeing. The Dinka people, for example, composed songs, naming dogs after stingy individuals. Individualism was foreign to the South Sudanese.

For the average thinker, myself included, we believe the South Sudanese people of today to be the same people they were yesterday. But we would be wrong to think this. Times have changed. Sometimes people are not generous; sometimes a South Sudanese will turn his or her head away. So if I were to begin the Walk in Honour trek with that assumption, that no matter how inadequate our finances we will always have someone supporting this project, I would be wrong. Allow me to explain.

Much of the change in attitude can be attributed to the recurring wars in the South Sudan. These wars have not only displaced people from their homes and villages but have also led to the introduction of foreign values including individualism. Over those years, the South Sudanese learned to envy another person's success. In the present time, they have become jealous and take no pride in anything good, learning only to be critical instead. The civil wars are to blame for this change in attitude and behaviour: the division, the hatred and the greed that now is rampant across all the territories and states of South Sudan. Ideas, whether they are benefiting a target group or have the potential to benefit the entire society directly or indirectly, are being rubbished or ignored. Corruption flourishes and those related to someone important will garner support. Ambivalence, indifference and suspicion meet any initiative put forward by an ordinary person. Social values to a large extent have been eroded.

Imagine if the Americans had been jealous of the Wright brothers. Would there be planes today? Would the lost boys of the Sudan ever have arrived in USA? What of Steve Jobs and his colleagues who put the internet in your pocket? I remember being ridiculed while promoting iHOPE on Facebook and attempting to explain how small initiatives could grow into well-regarded bodies such as World Vision, Save the Children Fund or ICRC. I read a comment from a lost boy, saying, this is a shame! That comment told me that either people are being intentionally negative or are suffering from low-self-esteem. Perhaps they cannot remember they were once tiny, short kids who gradually grew into tall boys and girls.

Whether we are driven by our desire to leave a legacy behind or by a passion for a cause we believe in, only a few of us actually do what it takes to accomplish a goal. Yet not every goal can be achieved. Our tendency to compare ourselves with other people can frustrate progress. Doubt sets in every time someone tells us that we will fail. Other people's advice or opinions can become ours and then we point fingers when we fail. That is the real shame. Our need to remain in our comfort zone can become more important than the benefit of small failings on the way to success.

Prior to undertaking the Walk in Honour, I was warned and cautioned about the perils awaiting me. I was reminded of the mysterious disappearance of tourists in the Australian outback and told to watch the Wolf Creek movie. I am not a movie fan and, sitting there hearing friends telling me about the death or disappearance of innocent citizens or visitors, was not helpful. Yet I remained more curious than afraid. Even as a child I remember wondering why someone would call it quits before even trying. I quietly began questioning why a sound person would kill a poor, skinny man like myself who has subjected himself to the scorching heat in the Northern Territory of Australia.

At the same time, I recalled my own past bad memories of wars, hunger and disease. I remembered assuming I was an orphan even when I was not. I remembered the near miss I had with death when a friend of mine, Deng Majiik (aka John Deng Atem Gak) and I were almost killed while searching for a friend in the jungles of Ethiopia. At the time, I couldn't imagine myself coming out alive again.

Whilst people laughed at the idea of walking 1500kms in seventeen days, there was one friend and co-worker who nodded approval but warned me of road trains, otherwise known as long trucks. Her name was Allison Mills and she advised me to keep a distance from the main highway as truckies or motorists could run me over. She warned that people had been killed on that highway and she was concerned for my safety. You see, inspiration can come in all kinds, shapes and sizes and what inspires one person may not inspire or even be noticed by another. That warning to keep a distance from the main highway only motivated and inspired me.

In the Invisible Giant novel, Bram Stoker wrote:

No longer was there the same love or the same reverence towards the king - no longer was there perfect peace. People had become more selfish and greedier and had tried to grasp all they could for themselves.

I believe love is an act rather just a word. I thought of all the little people caught in the maelstrom of South Sudan. At that time I wanted to give up my life for the orphans, the widows and the widowers, the disabled and the financial-disadvantaged, innocent family. I wanted to either walk myself to death or to endure because what mattered to me at the time was to achieve the goal I had set myself. I would not let the thrill of arriving in Alice Springs one morning be dampened by any imagined fear.

So the Walk in Honour began.

The Country of South Sudan

South Sudan, officially called the Republic of South Sudan, is one of the world's youngest countries, gaining its independence from the Republic of the Sudan in 2011. A land-locked country lying in East-Central Africa, its capital and largest city is Juba. It has a population of twelve million and half of these are under eighteen years of age. The dominant religion is Christianity.

For over four decades before independence, prolonged fighting had taken place between the northern Sudanese – who identify more with Arab culture - and the South Sudanese who identify more with African culture. Sadly, since the divide of Sudan and South Sudan, tensions have remained and a further civil war in South Sudan has seen this new country plunge further into chaos causing ongoing neglect, a lack

of infrastructural development, major destruction and displacement. As of 2017, despite not being ranked bottom in the latest UN World Happiness Report, it had the highest score on the American Fund for Peace's Fragile States Index (formerly the Failed States Index), surpassing Somalia.

Unfortunately, South Sudan's motto of *Justice, Liberty, Prosperity* falls way short of reality. The country is poverty-stricken and the ongoing wars have produced an appalling number of disadvantaged families, orphans, widows and disabled people. Rampant despair and poverty continue to escalate and cause additional 

problems such as street children, drug addiction, prostitution and very serious crime.

The South Sudanese orphans, widows and disabled feel utterly hopeless and they have always been homeless. They are the poorest of the poor. They continue to be born under trees, grow up under trees and die under trees. They have known only war. They are taught how to kill and the most beautiful thing in the world to them is a gun, because a gun may enable survival when confronted with the terror of the machine gun.

The United Nations High Commissioner for Refugees (UNHCR) has estimated that nearly one million people have fled from South Sudan into the neighbouring countries of Uganda, Sudan and Kenya, many being widows and orphans. However, a very large number of these marginalised people remain in South Sudan and comprise the majority of the country's vulnerable people.

South Sudan is once more in the cycle of killing and maiming and this renewed armed violence is producing even greater numbers of defenceless and vulnerable groups. To the South Sudanese, a man is not only the provider of food and security, he also provides a sense of belonging to his family.   Both children and their mother look to him, with hope, for purpose. With him gone, the family is defenceless and vulnerable, susceptible to all sort of insecurities including gang-rape, acquiring a sexually transmitted disease, chronic poverty and starvation.

Communicable diseases pose a major health threat in South Sudan and, consequently, are associated with significant levels of illness, death and disability. A lack of established health systems undermines any effective response to the largely preventable, infectious disease outbreaks. These outbreaks are driven by numerous factors caused by the current armed conflicts including displacement, overcrowding, poor sanitation and personal hygiene. All are aggravated by the poor environmental conditions.

World Health Organisation (WHO) estimated that approximately 12.6 million South Sudanese (the whole of South Sudan) are in great risk of disease outbreaks. In 2015 and 2016 alone, WHO reportedly responded to forty-nine disease outbreaks including cholera, malaria, measles, haemorrhagic viral fever and hepatitis across the entire country. Both cholera and malaria are major causes of illness and death in people of all ages, but are more prevalent in children's deaths. Malaria alone is a major contributing factor in countless miscarriages and stillbirths in many areas along the River Nile. Cases of measles and kala azar (visceral leishmaniasis or black fever) are also posing significant health concerns.

Proper and effective medical management of these diseases are contingent upon early and accurate detection. To boost the capacity for disease monitoring and response in South Sudan, iHOPE's long-term plan is to build a disease management complex comprising of diagnostics and public health research laboratories.

Some of the South Sudanese now living in Australia recall their early years of fear, struggle and flight:

Angelo Baak *Back days what a world of suffering*
Anthony King *We started from the bottom but now we here.*
Ayuel Deng Ayuel *Yes, It was really tough life but we managed to make a break through. I'm happy that some of us are alive to witness our suffering.*

Nyandeng Mawien *Amen*

Davidmalual Pandak *It was a long struggle with a lot of suffering during days in red army when we left our homes and joined SPLA to liberate the South Sudanese from Arab marginalisation. But some politicians put their individual interests before the nation.*

Stephen Malith Akook Wom, *I'm so happy to be a part of that toughest history of liberation struggle for independence of our country South Sudan. I'm very sure that photo was taken in 1991 in Korcuom after we left Ethiopia. Thanks you so much indeed Mr Daniel Ajak for posting that important picture.*

Augustino Deng *Yes, Ajakdit let those who are enjoying our blood's fruit see us in those days of struggle. We did suffered while they were resting and studies but now they are our masters in the government. Stephen Malith Akook We made the true history my lovely brother and best friend ever Daniel Ajak to liberate this country called South Sudan today despite all the unforgettable memories of too much pain and suffering which we thought our sacrifices would end, but unfortunately* *things fell apart. However, I still trust almighty God. He will grant us peace and love one day!*

Mathon Malek   *very suffering and so painful, may God BLESS you all.*

Manyang Agutyai recalls his South Sudanese experience:

- *The long barefoot walk by Red army comrades:*
- *It was only in 1992 some of the lost boys (Red Army) put on MuteKeli (car tyre shoes) for the first time. They are kind of shoes you wear until you die and leave behind.*
- *I hope the suffering the Red Army went through gave them a solid legacy that they left behind like MuteKeli for others to cherish. A legacy of coexistence, tolerance and patriotism.*
- *The Red Army walked barefooted from as far as Aweil to Ethiopia.*
- *The Red Army walked barefooted from as far as Dindinga Hills to Ethiopia.*
- *The Red Army walked barefooted from as far as Bentiu to Ethiopia.*
- *The Red Army walked barefooted from as far as from 99 Nuba mountains to Ethiopia.*
- *The Red Army walked barefooted from as far as Eastern Blue Nile to Ethiopia.*
- *The Red Army walked barefooted from many marginalised areas of the then Sudan to many points within and outside Sudan.*
- *The Red Army endured, hunger, many diseases, jingles, lack of shelters, homesickness, loneliness, hot sun, war and much more together regardless of tribe, clan, religion and region.*
- *The Red Army was the movement (SPLMA)'s social coexistence experiment. An experiment that, if successful, would mirror "The new Sudan" in which members of different regions could live side by side with ease.*
- *The Red Army at the time, was a great success. It is yet to be seen whether that previous success is still holding, now the young boys and girls of yesterday are cutting their political teeth in the turbulent political climate in South Sudan.*

- Being part of the barefooted walk, I would love to see my comrades wading carefully in the current muddy waters.

- We must be humble enough to acknowledge that we were not the only young kids of the time to have gone through such ordeals. Millions of young South Sudanese children went through the same ordeal in one way or another.

- I would love to see my comrades not falling into the trap of the liberators' sense of entitlement mode. Across the globe, clear-headed liberation struggles fall into chaos when a surviving few liberators are tempted to reward themselves at the expense of the objectives they took up arms for.

- As the Red Army, we are not entitled to anything more than any other South Sudanese. We are just members of the bigger South Sudan like all others.

- We are not special and we have not accomplished anything more than the average South Sudanese who donated his bull to feed the freedom fighters of the time. We are not entitled to anything more than a farmer who donated a sack of sorghum to feed the freedom fighters of the time. But we are better placed to fight the "liberators' sense of entitlement disease".

- It is so painful to see or hear that some Red Army comrades are thumping their chests about their roles in the liberation struggle. Some comrades even challenge others to prove their link to the Red Army.

- To me, this is a clear betrayal and unpatriotic. It is a clear indication that my comrades are likely to tread in the "liberators' sense of entitlement" path.

Kede Miäkduur   *Well said, brother.*

Bul Aguer-Ahoocjhok   *Well articulated Mr.Manyang Agutyai. Panchol Jol Alier Bless to all of us, who had endurance this horrible journey.*

Mathiang Garang Piok   *It is very sad memories comrade and long live Red Army groups as late Dr John Garang de Mabior said «the seeds of the nation South Sudan».*

Wen Sultan Alier Agutyai Manyangg   *that's why none of us don't want any intruders to rewrite the Red Army story in their own languages. It was a tiresome journey that none of us will forget.*

Bwana Mading   *It is an experience to be remembered by red army in their own lives. These are the type of things that we must invest our acquired western education in, rather than messing ourselves in those dirty politics we are currently engaging ourselves in South Sudan mr Agutyai. I wish you to keep on informing the red army on this line brother. I appreciate your contribution Manyangdit.*

Aleu Deng Bil   *Painful walk of survival to find safety has yield better results for the living. And our condolences to many of our brothers and sisters who perished during those agonising, sad, brutal, painful journeys. As a rememberance, your souls and memoirs are living with us and will be living with us forever because no child should ever have to sleep next to his brother's dead body, and no child should ever have to bury his own brother, friend, comrade, group or room-mate with sticks.*

Folks, I will leave there and I didn't meant to cause some physiological problems but treated as it is... the most brutal, sorrowful and painful journey of our lives. Thank you Agutyai Manyang for sharing it with the social networking families. It is a history by itself - a painful journey! Peace of Him Upstairs be with you all brothers and sisters.

What is iHOPE?

Integrated Help and Opportunities
for Peaceful Existence Incorporated

iHOPE Inc. is a registered charity in Australia, created in 2016, specifically to assist the families, widows, orphans and disabled of South Sudan. After fighting against oppression and injustice for over forty years, sadly some South Sudanese began committing the same oppression and injustices against their own people, the young, the old and the vulnerable.

Successfully addressing poverty and disadvantage in South Sudan requires an integrated approach. The iHOPE Inc. initiative is one such approach and strives to be a combination of projects purposely designed to empower and alleviate suffering.

iHOPE's overall goal is to improve the lives of the poorest and most marginalised groups through the provision of scholarships and vocational training. iHOPE believes that education is the key to achieving this goal because only education can help the poor escape the poverty cycle by developing the skills and knowledge needed to improve livelihoods.

iHOPE's vision is to create a better everyday life for financially disadvantaged families, orphans, widows and the disabled in South Sudan and also for their relatives here in Australia.

iHOPE strives to restore hope, dignity and self-reliance.

iHOPE presently supports this vision by offering access to scholarships and vocational training to the disadvantaged. This initiative has identified six key strategic priorities for its operations:

- Provide scholarships to financially-disadvantaged children
- Provide vocational training to widows and the disabled
- Build classrooms and purchase and provide equipment
- Advocate for financially-disadvantaged families and children
- Research, assess and evaluate iHOPE's impact so it may continue providing and delivering services and advocacy
- Participate and collaborate with other relief agencies on the ground in South Sudan working on the provision of emergency aid.

iHOPE's long-term plan is to build a disease management complex comprising of diagnostics and public health research laboratories.

Meet one of our beneficiaries

Meet Deng Bul

Mr Deng Garang Bul, also known as John Deng and Deng Adöör-Ayiik, is the President and CEO of iHOPE.

Deng has now worked in the non-profit sector For more than twenty years (since 1997) and continues today. Like all iHOPE's staff, he is a university postgraduate. A Medical Microbiologist and Public Health Researcher, Deng is a South Sudanese-Australian who is involved in charitable activities in the South Sudan's Jonglei State. He is the driving force behind iHOPE. Deng is a family man and father of lovely girls and a boy. He did not start well in life.

In 1987, when he was nine, he was separated from his parents and forced out by war with several other thousands of children his age. They fled South Sudan and trekked through jungles to Ethiopia where they spent the next four years. He slept, ate and studied under trees in Ethiopia. He survived the horrors of the jungle, not because he had a gun to protect himself, but because some kind people came to my assistance.

In Ethiopia he was clothed, fed, treated and educated by the UNHCR.

In 1991 he fled Ethiopia due to another civil war there. This time he trekked back across the border into South Sudan, then across another border, settling in the Kakuma refugee camp in north-eastern Kenya in 1992.

In 1993, at age fourteen, he made another dangerous journey back to South Sudan in an attempt to trace his family. Instead, he was recruited into the Sudan Liberation Army, the SPLA. With no means of escape he served for six years.

With the little education he had acquired, during this time he helped people whenever he could by working with relief agencies including the International Committee of the Red Cross (ICRC), MEDAIR and the Association of Christian Resource Organisation Serving Sudan (ACROSS).

Fortunately in 1997 he met aid worker, Doris Lempenauer, who worked with Medair. Through trust, compassion and a growing friendship, she offered to pay for his studies at a school in Kenya from 2001 through to 2004. Had he not met Doris, he could not predict what turns his life would have taken or even if he would still be alive today. He is a testimony to her generosity and kindness.

He migrated to Australia in 2004.

Although he partook involuntarily in that brutal civil war, he always hoped that one day, when the war was over, both regions of the Sudan would look back and establish peaceful societies where vulnerable people would be cared for and consoled.

Walk in Honour

Deng decided to do something dramatic to raise awareness of iHOPE and inject much needed capital into the charity.

It is more than thirty years since he fled South Sudan to a distant land but he remembers it clearly. He did not know what that trek would entail nor how hard it would be. Four years later, while living as an unaccompanied minor and refugee in Ethiopia, he realised that the ongoing hell he was experiencing could become a mission, a mission he came to admire and eventually would turn into a career.

He walked for two solid weeks at age nine, and repeated it again at thirteen, though this time for two months. Although he didn't know precisely how far he had walked, he counted the days and walked himself into freedom.

Therefore he decided to do it again. This time to WALK IN HONOUR and raise money for the afflicted, to WALK IN HONOUR of the homeless and fatherless children of South Sudan who must continue walking, trekking helplessly through their countryside seeking safety and a place they can call home.

Deng walked from Darwin to Alice Springs to honour all the men, women and children caught up in endless wars not of their making.

Preparation

Deng began promoting his walk and seeking sponsors in mid-April 2018 when he asked a reporter for NT News (Ms. Isabella Hood) to help publish a news article which she did on 1 May. The news article (*'Darwinite takes on Daring Walk'*) received some positive responses and he was encouraged by that. So he began planning for the actual walk by creating and publishing a Facebook page "Walk in Honour "on 15th May 2018.

Soon on board were CatholicCareNT, C3 Church in Darwin, and the Multicultural Council of the Northern Territory, along with many private individuals in the Darwin region. Members for Karama, Ngaree Ah Kit, Spillett, Lia Finocchiaro, NO MORE founder, Charlie King became a sponsor.

This picture was taken after the Walk in Honour planning meeting.

St John Ambulance NT donated a First Aid Kit.

Two Indigenous gentlemen from the Tiwi Islands offered to be Deng's support team. Uncle Frank (Emmanuel) Minniecon driving the support vehicle with Micah Wenitong at his side, documenting the walk. They were to go on ahead and prepare each evening's campsite and meal so that, when Deng arrived, he could simply eat and sleep and prepare for the following day.

Other early sponsors include:
Xavier College, Wurrumiyanga
Murrupurtiyanuwu Catholic School, Wurrumiyanga NT (also know as Bathurst Island or Nguiu)

Deng's Diary

Day 1: Monday 27 August

I began the Walk in Honour at 11 am, uncertain of what to expect and with whom I would cross paths.

I had planned to complete the walk in in seventeen days, arriving in Alice Springs on 13 September. However I soon had to revise this as it became obvious that it was too hot to walk through the middle of the day and I needed to rest during this time. However my second idea, to walk in the evenings and nights, presented other difficulties. A black man walking in the inky blackness of a tropical night along one of Australia's major highways was a disaster waiting to happen!

Someone asked me in Coolalinga why I was buying an NT map and was shocked when I mentioned I was walking to Alice Springs. That person even called me crazy, another word for insane, but am I? We will have the answer in two weeks. Stay cool.

Kevin Baxter-pilakui *Haha...The group was thinking the same tonight but wish u well*
U can do it mantani (Mantani means male friend in the Tiwi language)

I walked past many of the now abandoned airfields that were constructed during World War II for the defence of Darwin and Australia.

So I rested between midday and 3.30pm, then walked until sunset.

Sattler Airfield is an abandoned airfield that was constructed 32 km to the south of Darwin, Northern Territory, Australia during World War II. It is one of many airfields. On 2 April 1942, the then new Sattler RAAF airfield was bombed by the Japanese Imperial Forces.

Day 2: Tuesday 28 August

My second day begins very early. I feel fresh and strong for another push. Second stop for bush tucker. Was very yummy.

Walk In Honour   *Around Adelaide River*
Frances Ivinson   *Ok so far already*
Krissy Mulholland   *Good luck Deng hope you do very well.*

The Kungarrakan and Awarai Aboriginal peoples are acknowledged as the traditional owners of the land surrounding the present day town of Adelaide River. It is a small but historically important town, first settled by workers who arrived in the area to construct the Overland Telegraph Line. Adelaide River played a central role in the defence of Australia during the Second World War. In 1939, the town was designated as a rest area for personnel serving in Darwin, Northern Territory. In addition to many transient units, the 107th Australian General Hospital and 119th Australian General Hospital were set up within Adelaide River. The Adelaide River War Cemetery was established in 1942 following the Bombing of Darwin. It was used by the army field hospitals in the area to bury service personnel who were killed in action.

Day 3: Wednesday 29 August

You may not know how kind and caring road travellers and truckies are until you hit the road on your short, long, skinny or strong feet. A lot of drivers made the hardest U-turn and dangerous stops to ask me if I needed a lift. One of those who made a U-turn was surprised when I explained that I was walking for a charity and he gave me a skin care product. I believe he meant that my face would be shiny when I finished the walk.

Two other ladies, Dani and Martine who even did not know where in the world South Sudan is and what actually is happening in that country, were appreciative of the walk. Those girls will donate.

And the biggest of all are the truckies who treated me like a king. I love truckies and motorists. It is the iHOPE's world map folks. Have a good morning.

Pine Creek was traditionally the junction of three large indigenous ethnic groups. Stretching south-west from the Stuart Highway towards, and across, the Daly River was the land traditionally associated with the Wagiman people. The land east of the Stuart Highway and south of the Kakadu Highway, stretching to Katherine, was associated with the Jawoyn people, and north of the Kakadu Highway was land traditionally associated with Waray.

During construction of the Overland Telegraph line from Adelaide to Darwin in 1870, workers first crossed a creek that was notable for the pine trees that grew on its banks.

Day 4: Thursday 30 August

I have started the fourth day with crook ankles, hips and knees but with a revived spirit. Thanks to Uncle Frank Minniecon and Micah Wenitong who offered to walk on my behalf, but I reminded them that it is my walk!

Day 5: Friday 31 August

Fifth day into the walk. Good morning Katherine! 324 kms down already!

Beginning as an outpost established with the Australian Overland Telegraph Line on the North-South transport route between Darwin and Adelaide, **Katherine** has grown with the development of transport and local industries including mining – particularly gold mining; a strategic military function with RAAF Base

Tindal; also as a tourism gateway to the attractions of nearby Nitmiluk National Park, particularly Katherine Gorge and its many ancient rock paintings. The region is known to experience heavy flooding during the wet season.

Day 6: Saturday 1 September

Thank you Gerard Steele. Having read about the walk in Honour in NT News a week earlier, Mr. Gerard told me he never missed seeing me for the last three days while I was navigating my way through the hills of the Top End. Gerard was among those who waited under a tree to welcome me to Katherine today.

In addition to making a donation of money, Gerard leaves the following notes.

"Well done on your walk and efforts. Sudan needs help like many other developing countries. Turning violence and persecution to friendship and love is the way. All cultures- All colours- All CREEDS- we are all equals.

My special thank you also goes to Kuir Deng, (iHOPE's Treasurer) and Abuoi Dut (Abuja), see picture above, for spending their precious weekend to pay me a visit en-route. I owe you all the best wishes nature can extend to you. Thank you specifically to Abuja for your donation. It means a lot.

Amourchol Akuet *Well done wun akuach you are make us proud.*
Aduk Dau *Well done wun Akuach you are doing a wonderful job, good effort.*

Thank you very kindly Stanley Law of Australian Red Cross for the hearty welcoming to Katherine, free food and free accommodation. God will give you back in Abundance.

Day 7: Sunday 2 September

See you again soon Katherine!

Deng Bul, *And what is a Frilled neck lizard?*

Anne Hebert *Frilled neck lizard! It's the name of this lizard. Nice play on words NTG! Keep walking Deng, you are a legend!*

Day 8: Monday 3 September

Passing this sign reminds me of the recent cave rescue of the Thai Football team. It was a pleasant experience seeing the world coming together in response to their feelings.

Dave and his boys gave me XXXX. I hope Queenslanders know what this is! I never drank though because I did not want to get merry before a job done.

In the middle of highway's promoting iHOPE Inc. and NO MORE with Kerri of Rag Bags and Emma. Both ladies will donate. Thank you Emma and Kerri for being so kind.

And something sweet to refresh.

Dallas heard me talking on ABC radio while he was travelling to Alice

Springs and felt the need to support the Walk in Honour mission. A few days later Dallas saw me walking on the Stuart Highway and made a critical U-turn to make

sure he donated to the cause he is most interested in. A big thank you to Dallas for the donation. Thank you to those who are following the Walk in Honour Charity walk.

Made it to Mataranka, the capital of never never! 429 kms done!

Mataranka is a community of about 400, in the Top End. It is 107 km south of Katherine. At the 2011 census, Mataranka had a population of 244. The town is located near Roper River and Mataranka Hot Springs. This area is the setting for Jeannie Gunn's autobiographical account of the year 1902, "We of the Never Never". The homestead, which she shared with her husband, Aeneas Gunn, until his death, has been reconstructed near to the hot springs. The Australian Army set up No. 42 Australian Camp Hospital near Mataranka in World War II. The 10th Australian Advanced Ordnance workshops camped in buildings made from paper bark trees and serviced wrecked and damaged vehicles.

Thank you Rhonda and Henk Welter for your generous donation. Your feeling prevails over your other priorities. Thank you heaps.

Jok-Lual Alaak *Uncle, it is time to go home you had enough of NT desert Walk In Honour And where is home cousin?*
So my friend is telling me to go home? I was not sure about the home he meant, returning or Kiir Adhiok in South Sudan!! I do not know.

Day 9: Tuesday 4 September

Gorrie Airstrip is located 10 km north of Larrimah. Built during World War II it is reputed to be the largest, dirt airstrip in Australia. Gorrie was the largest army base in Australia during World War II and the airstrip was named after F/OP Peter C Gorrie, No. 2 Squadron RAAF who was killed in action near Menado, Dutch East Indies on 12 January 1942. Gorrie was used as the supply and maintenance depot for the defence against the Japanese and at the height of the war effort over 6,000 RAAF personnel were stationed in the area. They were all connected with stores, repair and replenishment for the aircraft flying sorties against the Japanese.

Larrimah is a tiny hamlet in the Northern Territory of Australia, approximately 428 kilometres southeast of Darwin. It has a population of 11. It is built along the Stuart Highway. It was the railhead

on the North Australia Railway during World War II. It is the home of the Big Stubby, a large replica of a Darwin Stubby beer bottle. The town›s pub was originally 9 km south in Birdum, but was moved when Larrimah became the end of the railway.

Day 10 & 11: Wednesday 4 September

Daly Waters. The area's traditional owners, the Jingili people, believe the Dreaming tracks of the Emu and the Sun travelled through here on their way to the southern parts of the Northern Territory. The name Daly Waters was given to a series of natural springs by John McDouall Stuart during his third attempt to cross Australia from south to north, in 1861-2.

Day 12: Wednesday 5 September

There are not many of them, but positive thinking individuals exist. Ross McGregor was told by his GP that he had only a short time to live and his response was, " I will go for a bike ride across Australia and I will be fine when I come back home. Ross comes from Victoria and he began riding his push bike in May 2018. So far he has covered

4,000 kms, but is looking fit and ever positive. Unlike me, Ross has no support team looking after him, so he has a metal box attached to his bike where his supply is maintained. I am not sure how much he's got in there but he did not seem to be concerned. If Ross is so positive despite his damning prognosis, why are we so negative about simple incidences?

That's how far we still have to go!

Dunmarra is a small settlement on the historical Overland Telegraph Line. Today, the town is little more than a roadhouse providing fuel, motel accommodation, a caravan park and other services to travellers. Drover Noel Healy established a cattle station here in the 1930s and discovered O'Mara's skeleton in the bush. The local Aboriginal people couldn't pronounce 'O'Mara', and their attempts sounded more like 'Dunmarra'. This lead Healy to the name of his station.

With me is Dominic, a Fairfax Media photographer who put aside his holiday fun to make sure that the iHOPE's mission reaches afar. Thank you Dom and Megan for being so receptive of our mission.

We arrived in Dunmarra and were welcomed by Missy Kelly Minaj. I may be wrong but our Africans here in diaspora usually do not like living in remote and rural areas, as if they actually come from cities, but Missy Kelly thrives there.

Thank you Kelly and family for the hospitality you showed us. Thank you very kindly for the finest, delicious free food. Uncle Frank and Micah continued to be impressed by your kindness and level of your generosity.

Frankly, I was little emotional as I have no African involved with me in this walk. However you became one and I understood that you also would have wanted to undertake a physical walk if you did not have a baby to care for. You have already done your part sister. Thank you from the bottom of my heart. My friends whom I am bonded with not by relationship but by love, feeling and humanity are all wishing you the very best.

I pray that God, the giver, gives to you in abundance. You have given to orphans and other vulnerable people in South Sudan and that cannot be taken lightly.

Missy Kelly Minaj *You doing a great job*
Palesa Lolo Ditau *Awwwww Missy Kelly Minaj this is beautiful, you have an amazing heart. This right here...a blessing.*
Walk In Honour *Blessing from the most high. He is so generous.*

Day 13: Saturday 8 September

Honouring individuals because of what they have achieved for the people advances the world.

There is a monument to the Overland Telegraph Line beside the Stuart Highway south of Dunmarra, dedicated to Sir Charles Todd, Postmaster, General of the Province of South Australia, 1872.

Day 14: Sunday 9 September

Newcastle Waters is a deserted small settlement off the Stuart Highway, virtually uninhabited except for visitors. It is inside Newcastle Waters Station, a large cattle station with over 40,000 head of cattle.

Sleeping under the stars and sunrise south of Newcastle Waters on WALK IN HONOUR with Deng Bul and Uncle Frank. 720kms down.

Day 15: Monday 10 September

Elliott is a town in Northern Territory, Australia. It is almost halfway between Darwin and Alice Springs on the Stuart Highway. The town is in the Yapurkulangu ward of the Barkly Region. The area is the home of the Jingili people and the traditional name of the town is Kulumindini. At the 2006 census, Elliott had a population of 355.

The town began at the site of Number 8 Bore on Newcastle Waters Station as an Australian Army camp during World War II. It is named after Army Captain R.D (Snow) Elliott MBE.

Elliott is on the edge of the Newcastle Waters Station and is 23 kilometres (14 mi) from Newcastle Waters, a town near the station homestead and at the junction of three important stockroutes.

Day 16: Tuesday 11 September

At a small but accommodating Roadside house called Renner Springs Desert Inn, was there a quote which I would like to share with you from the onset. It reads "How far we travel in life matters far less than those we met along the way."

Renner Springs is named after Dr Frederick Renner, he was the Doctor to the men working on the Overland Telegraph Line in 1871. Dr

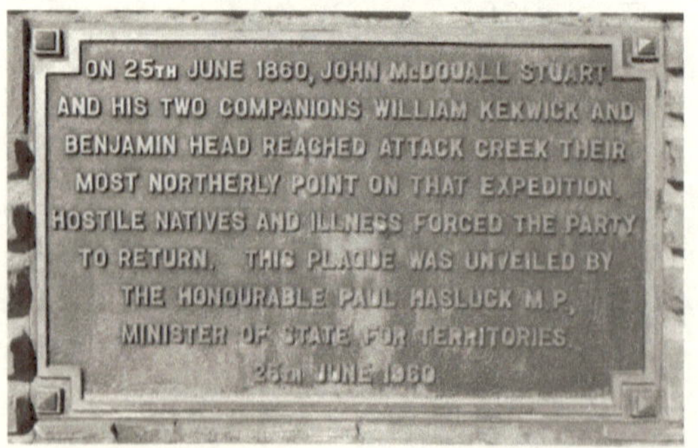

Renner's diary records a large gathering of birds and while investigating he discovered the Mud Springs. The Mud Springs can still be seen by an enjoyable walk and the large Lagoon

still support a large range of the Territory's natural birdlife.

The Attack Creek Memorial is situated on the **Attack Creek Historical Reserve**, located on the Stuart Highway 74 kilometres north of Tennant Creek. A short walk down the creek from the monument you can see where the old Stuart Highway once ran to the east of the current road.

Day 18: Thursday 13 September

Good morning. I went straight instead of going left.

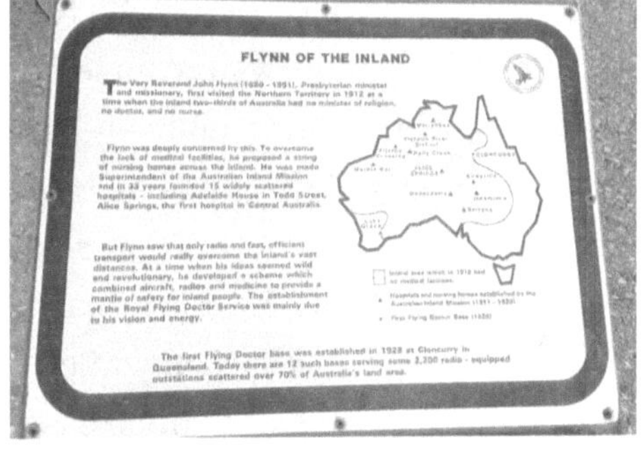

The **Three Ways Roadhouse** and Tourist Park is situated on the corner of Barkly & Stuart Highways and is a convenient stop for travellers heading North, South or East. The Roadhouse first sold fuel in the 1960's from 44 gallon drums!

It is 25 kilometres north of Tennant Creek. A local point of interest is the **Flynn Memorial**. Reverend John Flynn pioneered the Royal Australian Flying Doctors Service. The memorial originally sat at the exact meeting spot of the Barkly and Stuart Highways, but the point has now been moved 250 metres south.

Tennant Creek has a population of approximately 3,000, of which over 50% (1,536) identified themselves as Indigenous.

The town is approximately 1,000 kilometres south of the territory capital, Darwin, and 500 kilometres north of Alice Springs. It is named after a nearby watercourse of the same name, and is the hub of the sprawling Barkly Tableland vast elevated plains of black soil with golden Mitchell grass, that cover more than 240,000 square kilometres. Tennant Creek is also near well-known attractions including the Devils Marbles, Mary Ann Dam, Battery Hill Mining Centre and the Nyinkka Nyunyu Culture Centre

The Barkly Tableland runs east from Tennant Creek towards the Queensland border and is among the most important cattle grazing areas in the Northern Territory. Roughly the same size as the United Kingdom or New Zealand, the region consists largely of open grass plains and some of the world's largest cattle stations. It runs as far south as Barrow Creek, north above Elliott and west into the Tanami Desert.

I arrived in Tennant Creek at around noon. That concludes the second leg of the Walk in Honour. Here I spoke to the students at Tennant Creek High School about my walk and the aims of iHOPE. I told them nothing is impossible if you are committed and you care. I urged them to put an end to violence and drugs and start to do good in the world – by doing small things, to make a better world.

Another reason to walk was to inspire our young people who are being bombarded day in day out with impossibilities. Love or a yummy dinner is no longer an easy way out for the dotcom generation but a frank talk from an inspiring dad or mum is the remedy. Their questions were ranging from what my favourite shoes or music was to how possible it was to walk 1500kms. I told the students I had no favourite and impossible was not in my vocabularies, simply because I was unwilling to get stuck. I understand things can be hard but not impossible to do. A favourite means no alternative, which is silly. Young people are conditioned to accept other people's opinions as theirs and this too needs to be eradicated.

Enjoying precious moments with brother Michael Nyieth (aka Dador) and Uncle Frank just before we head off to Alice Springs. Thank you Michael for the warm welcoming to Tennant Creek and huge support. We look forward see you back soon.

Day 19: Friday 14 September

Morning folks. I have the honour to extend our gratitude to Maker Mayek for his unyielding support for the iHOPE cause. Thank you my friend for being there for us all.

Maker Mayek *No worries brother. It's my pleasure to assist to amplify the message. I hope it goes well. You've put your body on the line for a great cause and I wish you nothing but success.*

I visited the Barkly Regional Council in Tennant Creek and spoke to the mayor, Mr. Steven Edgington, telling him about iHOPE and its aim to provide aid to children from financially disadvantaged families including Australian families, South Sudanese civil war orphans, widows and the disabled in need. I told him I had walked from Darwin to Tennant Creek as part of the Walk In Honour charity to raise money for disadvantaged children and asked if he would sponsor the walk for charity.

On Friday, **Mr Deng Bul**, *the CEO and Charity Manager of IHOPE Inc visited the Barkly Regional Council.*
The integrated Help and Opportunities for Peaceful Existence

(iHOPE) Inc. *provides aid to children from financially disadvan-taged families including Australian families, South Sudanese civil war orphans, widows and the disabled in need.*

Deng has walked from Darwin to Tennant Creek as part of the Walk In Honour charity walk raising money for disadvantaged children. He visited our office to see if Council would sponsor their purpose. A humble and quiet man who asked for nothing more than food and water to aid their groups walk to Alice Springs.

The Barkly Regional Council contributed a small donation of $200.00 to the organisation by purchase order to IGA from Youthlinks.

They were very thankful and Deng will return at some stage to talk to the children at Youthlinks about the importance and privilege it is to have an education.

For more information about iHOPE *please visit www.ihope.org.au*

We look forward to seeing Deng back in Tennant Creek soon.

- Steven Edgington

We are thankful to Barkly Regional Council for their support for the Walk in Honour and I promised to return at some stage to talk to the children at Youthlinks about the importance and privilege it is to have an education. We look forward to return toTennant Creek soon.

Day 20: Saturday 15 September

Thanks Greg and the Devils Marbles management for the free delicious meals, coffee and hot showers for the Walk in Honour gents. Yours was a great service.

Day 20: Saturday 16 September

Although Wycliffe Well only has a few permanent inhabitants, many travellers can't miss it while driving on the Stuart Highway from or to the Red Centre. In Australia, a small settlement like this is known as a roadhouse, a service stop for gas, food and accommodation for long drives through the Outback.

But Wycliffe Well is not just another roadhouse — it is the self-proclaimed UFO Capital of Australia. According its own brochure, "UFO sightings are so common, that if you stayed up all night looking, you would be considered unlucky not to see anything, rather than lucky to see something".

The Central Desert Regional Council is a local government area of the Northern Territory, Australia. The Council's main towns are Ti Tree, Yuendumu and Lajamanu. The Region covers an area of 282,090 square kilometres (108,916 sq mi) and had a population of over 3,500 people as at the 2016 Census.

Day 22: Sunday 17 September

Thank you to Michael and staff, at Barrow Creek, for your support on WALK IN HONOUR. We are 280 Km to Alice Springs.

For most of its history Barrow Creek has been an isolated and tiny outpost on the Stuart Highway north of Alice Springs. Then, on

14 July 2001, it became a vital part of one of the Australian outback's most horrific and mystifying crimes. On the night of 14 July, Bradley John Murdoch stopped a VW Kombi van driven by English traveller, Peter Falconio, and persuaded Falconio to leave the vehicle, shot him, tied up Falconio's girlfriend Joanne Lees who, miraculously, managed to escape, hide in the scrub along the highway, and was eventually picked up by a truck driver who took her 13 km south to the Barrow Creek pub where the police were alerted.

Day 23: Wednesday 18 September

Emily Gullberg Lundblad *recommends* Walk In Honour. *We are so lucky to have this kind of people in our World! Please try to take care of each other and help people in need!!   it's just so beautiful.*

Ti Tree is a tiny settlement. Its main claim to fame is that it is the closest settlement to Central Mount Stuart, the geographical centre of Australia. The land around Ti Tree is flat and inhospitable. The Reynolds Ranges in the south-west and the Watt Ranges in the north-east only break the flatness.

Passing Anmatjere Woman and Child at Aileron, 70kms north of Alice Springs. Anmatjere Man is also there, standing on top of the hill in all his warrior splendour, giving a glimpse of the great Aboriginal spirit in this country.

Rick Withapee LOOKS LIKE DINKA
Joy Stevenson *Congratulations!*

Day 23: Wednesday 19 September

Micah and I slept around this fire, but Uncle Frank was dreaming inside the car. He called Mattress. Thought he was homesick!!!!

Last camp fire

Day 24: Thursday 20 September

Our last road camp!

Day 25, Friday 21 September

Approaching Alice Springs and THE END!! Looking down into Alice Springs.

I arrived in Alice Springs feeling great and excited. I had met many wonderful people on the way and had accepted no lifts. People had called me crazy but, after twenty-five days of walking, I was finally here!

Alice Springs (Arrernte: Mparntwe) is the third-largest town in the Northern Territory of Australia. Popularly known as "the Alice" or simply "Alice", Alice Springs is situated roughly in Australia's geographic centre. The area is known as Mparntwe to its original inhabitants, the Arrernte, who have lived in the Central Australian desert in and around what is now Alice Springs for tens of thousands of years. The name Alice Springs was given by surveyor William Whitfield Mills after Alice, Lady Todd (née Alice Gillam Bell), wife of the telegraph pioneer Sir Charles Todd.

The town straddles the usually dry Todd River on the northern side of the MacDonnell Ranges. The surrounding region is known as Central Australia, or the Red Centre, an arid environment consisting of several different deserts.

Warmest reception at CatholicCare NT in Alice Springs. Thank you CCNT staff for making me feel so much at home. Thank you all for your support and love!! "How far we travel in life matters far less than those we met along the way."

Rodney Halligan   *Awesome!!!...........congratulations Deng!!!!*
Walk In Honour Rodney Halligan ,   *I have met several people on push bikes along Stuart highway and I thought they were doing it tough than I was doing.*
A flat land would be a good walk!!!
Maria Beraldo   *Deny you are an inspiration well done.*
Anyieth Arou Maan   *Congratulations*
Hopkins Helen   *Well done*
Anne Hebert   *You made it!!! What a champ you are!!!*
Alek Dhieu Atem   *Waw! He is one in a million to made it*
Aguer Garang Bul   *Congratulations brother for that great achievement. Hard work and determination never go unrewarded. Keep the pot boiling for the orphans to smile.*
Riak Deng   *Amazing sweathreat you deserve it.*
Ove Rasmussen Kjaer   *Fantastic.*
Missy Kelly Minaj   *Great job, Mate.*

Rodney Halligan   *great commitment Deng............you and Ove's names will always be in Australian history now!!!*

Chrys Benson   *A job well done, Deng. You are a star, and the compassion you have is an inspiration for many others. To never give up on one soul all alone out there.*

David Chol   *Great job*

Day 26 Saturday 22 September

Recovering in Alice Springs

Please join me tomorrow at 9.30 am NT local time for a thank you Facebook live video to those who have been following the Walk in Honour trek. If that appeals to you then I would like to have a chat with you to say thank you and be friends indefinitely.

Deng Bul: Memories are more than initial actions since they revive goals and directions. Thank you to NT News for your tireless commitment in promoting the iHOPE Inc. Thank you to Teghan Hughes from CAAMA for interviewing me and spreading the iHOPE message.

After the Walk

We began the Walk in Honour not certain about what to expect or who we could cross paths with. However as the crazy trek (as referred to by some) unfolded and the reality sat in, a memorable experience emerged. So today it is not how far we/I have travelled that matters but the people I met and shared my experiences with that matters.

I came across real people-those who care and were courageous enough to pat me at the back and said well done! It is a good cause. I have been accommodated and fed free of charge. Yet others showed me with words such as "You are my champion, my hero, you are an inspiration to me." Those positive words and phrases pushed me along the way.

Initially, though not to me, the Walk in Honour did sound like a joke to most people but was appreciated and encouraged by a few nonetheless. Some people wondered if I was out of my mind and a few jokingly said I was crazy. I spoke to multitudes in a wide range of careers including politicians, media, the police and the members of local government but not many believed it would actually happen.

It was a learning experience for me. Just to hear negative remarks from people whom we expected to inspire us was devastating. I was invited to deliver talks to students and youth along the way, however sometimes they still could not believe what they were seeing.

That is the mindset which has been imposed on us by those who think they care. That some undertakings are impossible while only a small proportion thought it workable. Think about that! A world where we limit ourselves to do the usual because others have told us that what we aim for and believe in is impossible! "Should" is an enemy. Trust me. I met Ross McGregor who was told by his doctors that he had a short time to live, but his response was, "I will go for a bike ride and when I return home, I will be fine." How about adopting that positive attitude? How much money do we need to spend to change our mindset?

Honestly this walk was a personal experience for me in that I had to redefine friend, friendship and community. At some point I wondered where my community was, but then Michael Nyieth (aka Dador) yelled out and said "I have your back brother." Also, unexpectedly, Missy Kelly Minaj appeared with a smile. Even at the time when the rest of Australians, young and not so young, rich and not so rich, celebrated my arrival in Alice Springs I was still wondering if actually my community would appear somewhere. Only Stephen Odusa emerged and told me, "Brother, here I am." Stephen shed tears of joy and nostalgia. I owe you, Stephen.

Are we there folks?

Thank you to those who made the Walk in Honour their own. A BIG thank you goes to **CatholicCare NT** who gave it their all to make sure not only would I cross the finish line but also come back home sound and intact. I am back home healthier, sound and kicking.

Thank you to the **Multicultural Council of the Northern Territory** who worked in partnership with the iHOPE Inc. My walk shoes never worn out. I understand partnership better now after you offered to help me with the Walk in Honour. Thank you MCNT.

Thank you to **C3 Darwin**, you are not only my spiritual home but the iHOPE Inc birthplace.

Thank you to **Barkly Regional Council** for the warm welcome and generous donation. We have no better friend than the town of Tennant Creek.

Thank you to the Media-NT News, the ABC radio, TEABBA radio, SBS Dinka Radio and CAAMA media who welcomed me to the rocky town of Alice Springs. Thank you to Stuart Highway travellers, the truckies, motorists and motorcycles, the campers, the caravans and roadside houses who accommodated and fed me free of cost, and the service stations amongst others. The sound of horns and thumbs up were sweet. I owe you more.

Thank you also to Charlie King of **NO MORE** and the **Wurrumiyanga Catholic Schools**.

Thank you to individuals - including Dell Brand the iHOPE Inc. Editor, Kate Worden (donor), member for Sanderson, Ngaree member for Karama, Lia member for Spillet, Jane Lloyd, Jean Ah Chee, Christian Metzger, Rohan Smyth, Maker Mayek, Chol Bol Ayuen (iHOPE's Vice president), Garang Malual Jok (donor) and family, Thon Ayii, Dominic Lorimer of Fairfax media and Akuar Dut of SBS Dinka for amplifying the message of iHOPE.

Thank you to all those who have and continue to donate their money and time to the Walk in Honour, for you are the backbone of this project. You are my champions.

Thanks to the iHOPE Inc team who encouraged and supported me both as a team and individually. Thank you to the South Sudanese families in the Darwin, who spared their precious time to farewell and wish me well in my last ordeal.

My special thank you goes to my family - to my dearest wife, Riak Deng Aleu, and to my dearest children Akuach, Ajoh, Ayak, Amou (Emma) and little man Garang (Garang Jnr). I love you all. And to siblings, Aguer Manyuon, Bul Mawan, Achol (Nyandior) Dau, Dengs junior, Ayiik-Malek and my parents who thought something bad would befall me. I am alive and sane.

To relatives and friends who struggled to understand what the merits of the last walk were. I am back home.

Sometimes we grapple with or cannot grasp what friendship means or who are our truest friends. If you put yourself into something unusual, you will not fail to know who they are. If you have just met them and they believe in you and stick with you in unusual places, then look no further, you have found them. Uncle Frank Minniecon and Micah Wenitong are my truest brothers and friends. Thank you Frank and Micah! He who blesses and gives abundantly is always on your side.

If you have just completed a task dear to your heart and you yearn for more or wonder what's next for you, then you are alive. It began on the left and probably ended on the right, but it has never ended. Thank you all. May God bless you!!

Ove Rasmussen Kjaer   *Powerful words. Congratulations.*

Agou Anyieth Kur.   *To only say congratulation my friend* **Deng Bul** *would be an understatement. However what you have accomplished through the "walk in Honour" is very noble. With great strides, sacrifice and determination, you have put purpose and dignity to the plight of the people of South Sudan. Proud of your achievement my friend!*

Pastor Lars Halvorsen   *Drawing inspiration from his own journey, Deng is a selfless and dedicated advocate for the children of South Sudan.*

This is someone else cherishing my achievement.

But do not think that I posted this certificate on Facebook because it matters greatly to me. I am simply honouring CCNT leadership and staff for their continuing show of support. Thank you to CatholicCare NT Berrimah for hosting the breakfast in honouring my trek. It makes me wonder if someone else makes what I felt like solely mine; my own ordeal their joy. What would the world look like if we can all do it? A better world? A gloomy world? What would your world be? Mine is absolutely hopeful.

Back Home

Greet the iHOPE's new arrivals

On behalf of these boys' families and relatives, iHOPE Inc. wishes to extend its gratitude to Ms Helen Hopkin of Caboolture Christian Children's Centre for sponsoring Deng and Dau. Thank you Ms Hopkins for your kindness and care. Your work is nothing other than the restoration of HOPE to hopeless South Sudanese children and their families.

Hopkins Helen *We are so happy to be able to be able to support these boys and pray for their future. This is something that we are happy to do together as a team at Caboolture Christian Children's Centre.*
Amero Jojo De Garang *Ur highly welcome home God blesses u*
Agou Anyieth Kur *Congratulation my friend Deng Garang for a great challenge you undertook. Very proud of you.*

Jok-Lual Alaak *Welcome back John de Baptist. Walking over 1500 kilometers in a desert like environment of NT was a torture in it totality. This is an achievement a media does not want to cover because it is not about Melbourne gang anymore. Like thousand miles we walked in rough days of our liberation, you have once again took the challenge in an environment where KFC and McDonalds demanded our blood. Send that little dollars to South Sudan for war reconstruction efforts. No more trekking of thousand miles on feet. Above all, I thank Almighty God for protecting you throughout thin and thick of your desired mission, Deng Bul*

Ador Bul-makuol *You are highly welcome back home that is great.*

David Piok *Raan thii yin cie luoidu looi, acie ke beere monydit leu.*

Micah Wenitong *You are a Champion mr Deng Bul Well done!!!*

So what next?

I have been asked numerous times by relatives, friends and acquaintances that what next for you now that you have completed your big walk? We all have challenges facing us in our day to day life and the above question continues to bother me a great deal. However allow me to answer you with direct quote.

It says. "We must have a theme, a goal, a purpose in our lives. If you don't know where you're aiming, you don't have a goal. My goal is to live my life in such a way that when I die someone can say, she cared. Mary Kay Ash. So my next goal is to keep caring for those who need my care.

Footnote

Walk in Honour's donations are still ongoing but presently the amount raised has been around $5000. If you spend that $ purchasing this booklet you are restoring hope to the hopeless.

Find us

www.ihope.org.au

www.dengbul.com

Follow us on the Facebook at Facebook.com/ihope16

Walk in Honour Foundation

PO BOX 41538

Casuarina NT 0810

E: **info@ihope.org.au**

E: **deng.bul@outlook.com.au**

Mob: 0400211966